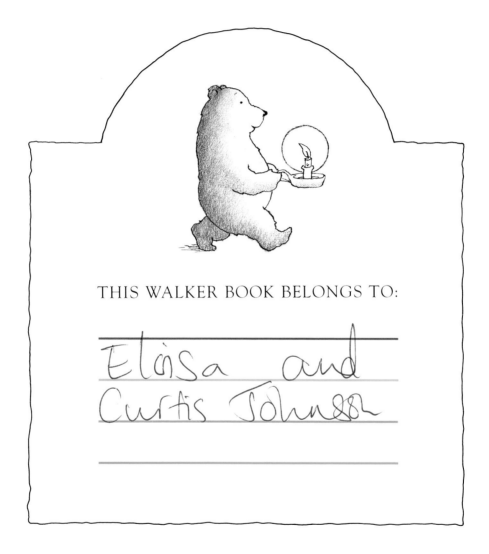

THIS WALKER BOOK BELONGS TO:

Eloisa and
Curtis Johnson

For Noreen
M.W.

First published 1989 by Walker Books Ltd
87 Vauxhall Walk, London SE11 5HJ

This edition published 2002

4 6 8 10 9 7 5 3

Text © 1989 Martin Waddell
Illustrations © 1989 Barbara Firth

The right of Martin Waddell and Barbara Firth to be identified as
author and illustrator respectively of this work has been asserted by
them in accordance with the Copyright, Designs and Patents Act 1988

This book has been typeset in Times

Printed in China

British Library Cataloguing in Publication Data:
a catalogue record for this book is available from the British Library

ISBN 0-7445-9408-1

www.walkerbooks.co.uk

The Park in the Dark

Martin Waddell
illustrated by Barbara Firth

WALKER BOOKS
AND SUBSIDIARIES
LONDON · BOSTON · SYDNEY · AUCKLAND

When the sun goes down
and the moon comes up
and the old swing creaks
in the dark,
that's when we go
to the park,
me and Loopy
and Little Gee,
all three.

Softly down the staircase,

through the haunty hall,

trying to look

small,

me and Loopy

and Little Gee,

we three.

It's shivery
out in the dark
on our way to the park,
down dustbin alley,
past the ruined mill,
so still,
just me and Loopy
  and Little Gee,
    just three.

And Little Gee
doesn't like it.
He's scared
of the things
he might see
in the park
in the dark
with Loopy and me.
That's me and Loopy
and Little Gee,
the three.

There might be
moon witches
or man-eating trees
or withers that wobble
or old Scrawny Shins
or hairy hobgoblins,
or black boggarts' knees
in the trees,
or things we can't see,
me and Loopy
  and Little Gee,
    all three.

But there's not,

says Loopy,

and I agree,

and Little Gee

gets up on my back and

we pass the Howl Tree,

me and Loopy

  and Little Gee.

    We're heroes,

     we three.

In the park

in the dark

by the lake

and the bridge,

that's when we see

where we want to be,

me and Loopy

and Little Gee.

WHOOPEE!

And we swing

and we slide

and we dance

and we jump

and we chase

all over the place,

me and Loopy

and Little Gee,

the Big Three!

And then

the THING comes!

YAAAAA

AAAIII

OOOOOEEEEEEE!

RUN RUN RUN
shouts Little Gee
to Loopy and me
and we
flee,
me and Loopy
and Little Gee,
scared three.

Back where we've come

through the park

in the dark

and the THING

is roaring

and following,

see?

After me and Loopy

and Little Gee,

we three.

Up to the house,
to the stair,
to the bed
where we ought to be,
me and Loopy
and Little Gee,
safe as can be,
all three.